This book belongs to:

_____

GROSSET & DUNLAP
An Imprint of Penguin Random House LLC, New York

Copyright © 2020 by Penguin Random House LLC. Based on the book THE LITTLE ENGINE THAT COULD (The Complete, Original Edition) by Watty Piper, illustrated by George & Doris Hauman, © Penguin Random House LLC. The Little Engine That Could®, I Think I Can®, and all related titles, logos, and characters are trademarks of Penguin Random House LLC. All rights reserved. Published by Grosset & Dunlap, an imprint of Penguin Random House LLC, New York. GROSSET & DUNLAP is a registered trademark of Penguin Random House LLC. Manufactured in China.

Visit us online at www.penguinrandomhouse.com.

Library of Congress Cataloging-in-Publication Data is available upon request.

ISBN 9780593094570
10 9 8 7 6 5 4 3 2 1

The Little Engine That Could®

# Good Night, Little Engine

by Janet Lawler

illustrated by Jill Howarth

Grosset & Dunlap

Little Engine played all day.
It's time for bed. She's in her bay.

The train yard's still. There's not a sound.
The setting sun glows all around.

But Little Engine's wide awake.
How much longer will it take

for her to settle down to sleep,
counting cars instead of sheep?

Then Little Engine
hears a noise—

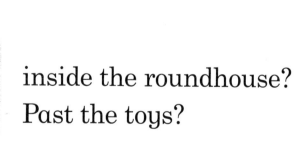

inside the roundhouse?
Past the toys?

She inches out to take a look
in every stall and shadowed nook.

She hears the sound again, outside.

Curious, she takes a ride.

"Peep! I tumbled from my nest.
I'm lost! Please help. Which way is best?"

Little Engine says, "Oh dear!
I'll help you, Birdie. Have no fear."

She peers inside the nearest tree.
"No nest in here that I can see."

So Little Engine wakes a friend.
Rusty Engine rounds the bend.

He searches down another track.
"No bird home here!" He circles back.

Little Engine rouses toys—
the monkey, dolls, and soldier boys.

They look in boxcars,
down the line.

Giraffe explores
the ticket sign.

TICKETS

They check the poles
and storage shed.

No nest in sight.
No birdie bed.

Then Little Engine gives a yawn.
"Birdie, stay with us till dawn."

Birdie nods. His feathers droop.
At least he's found this friendly group.

They troop inside the roundhouse door,
where high above the track-filled floor,
they hear loud chirps and peeps and cries.

"*Mama?!*" Birdie blinks his eyes.
"It's me!" chirps Birdie. "Coming, now!"
But then he stops and wonders, *How?*

His wings will only flap and fan.
Little Engine says, *"WE CAN!"*

The friends stack up and Birdie hops
to climb them all and reach the top.

The nest is still a bit too high.
Giraffe's the last to give a try.

She settles Birdie in his nest.
"There you go. It's time to rest."

"Thanks," sings Birdie, snuggled tight
and safe with Mama for the night.

Below, the toys share bedtime hugs.
Little Engine smiles and chugs.

"I *knew* we could," she says out loud
to all the weary train yard crowd.

"We *knew* we could!" they whisper back
as dreams descend along the track.

*Good night, Little Engine!*